Saving Jackson's Tooth

Written by Dr. Jeff Shnall
Illustrated by Catherine Lee

First paperback edition June 2019

Book design by Catherine Lee
Cover design by Catherine Lee

ISBN 978-1-9991101-0-9 (paperback)
ISBN 978-1-9991101-2-3 (ebook)
ISBN 978-1-9991101-1-6 (hardcover book)

Published by Beech Avenue Publishing

www.BeechAvenuePublishing.com

Disclaimer

This is a work of fiction. Names, characters, places, and incidents either are the product of the author's imagination or are used fictitiously. Any resemblance to actual persons, living or dead, events, or locales is entirely coincidental.

However, Sugar Bugs will surely eat holes in your teeth if left unchecked. See your dentist regularly! As well, the author does not recommend children tie their loose baby teeth to objects animate or inanimate for the purpose of tooth removal, and again should consult either their parent or dentist for assistance.

Saving Jackson's Tooth

Written by Dr. Jeff Shnall
Illustrated by Catherine Lee

Jackson just turned six years old.
Birthdays are such fun!
But if you look inside his mouth,
A party has begun.

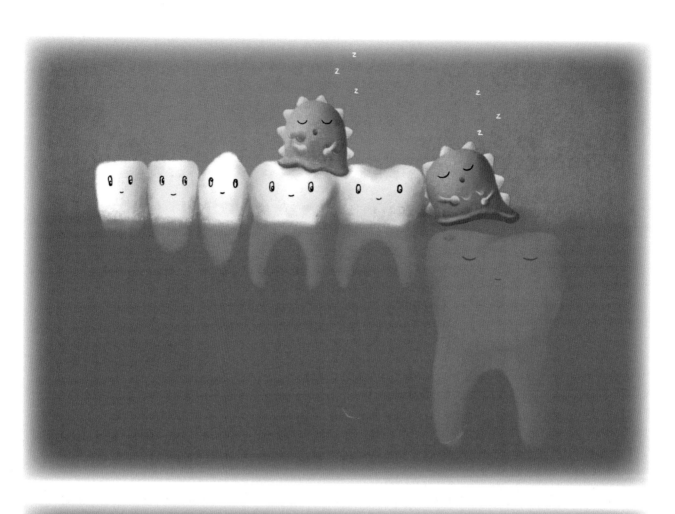

His baby teeth wore silly hats.
There were streamers hanging too.
But what would teeth be celebrating?
The picture holds a clue.

"Welcome," said a baby tooth.
"You've finally arrived.
A new big molar for Jackson.
And my, you're supersized!

"The rest of us are baby teeth,
We only last so long.
But you, my friend, are permanent
If you stay clean and strong."

But another baby tooth then said,
"There's something I must mention.
You have a big hole in your head
That needs your prompt attention."

"That can't be," said the molar.
"I'm practically brand new."
Well, sometimes teeth grow in with flaws.
Unfortunately, it's true.

It was now piñata time,
So Jackson gave a whack.
"Oh no!" said a baby tooth.
"A Sugar Bug attack!"

Jackson ate the candy
That spilled out on the floor.
But this woke up the Sugar Bugs
Who all lined up for more.

"Sugar Bugs?" asked the molar.
"What is it that they do?"
"They're little pests that grow on teeth
And stick to us like glue.

"They eat sugar and poop out acid
That can turn a tooth to mush.
They hide in little holes in teeth
That kids find hard to brush."

A baby tooth continued,
"I've got other news for you.
When Sugar Bugs get bigger,
They can split themselves in two.

"They split again and split again
Until a few becomes a lot.
If Jackson doesn't brush them off
Then you and I could rot."

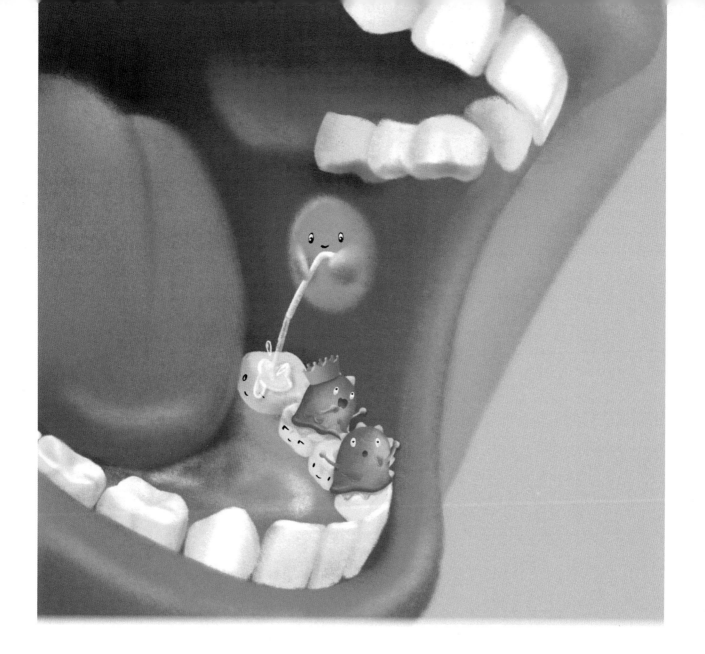

"Hey, don't forget we're here to help,"
Said the Dribble Slobber Glands.*
"We squirt saliva onto teeth
And we drool upon command.

"We wash off Sugar Bugs
And we spray calcium on you,
To fill the holes made by acid
And keep you good as new."

*The Dribble Slobber Glands are actually the salivary glands.

"This hole in my head," said the molar,
"I don't feel it much at all.
Let's leave it. If it bothers me,
I'll give you guys a call."

"Nonsense," said a baby tooth.
"You need to know the truth.
Sugar Bugs will invade that hole
And eat deep down in the tooth.

"And if the hole is not repaired
You could break right in two.
We need to get you to a dentist.
It's the smartest thing to do."

"Let's just ask Jackson," said the molar,
"To give his dentist a call."
"That's not easy," said the baby tooth.
"He can't hear our voice at all.

"But every time we speak,
Jackson's dog Doodles is aware.
Hey Doodles, if you hear us
Raise your ears up in the air."

Two whole months have passed.
The hole in Jackson's tooth has grown.
It's a rather nasty cavity.
We wish Jackson's folks had known.

At breakfast Jackson said, "Oh wow!
My baby tooth just moved.
And the Tooth Fairy surely visits kids
Once it is removed.

"Maybe she can come tonight.
There's no need to delay.
I'll take this loose tooth out myself.
I think I know a way."

With one end of string tied to his tooth,
The other to the door,
Jackson called out to his sister, "Mia!"
You should have heard him roar!

Mia came running lightning fast
And pushed hard on his door.
And when she burst into his room,
His tooth was on the floor.

"What's the matter?" Mia asked,
While looking quite confused.
Jackson said, "You pulled my tooth!"
And she was not amused.

That very night the Tooth Fairy
Fluttered over Jackson's bed,
When she heard a tiny voice,
For a baby tooth had said,

"Tooth Fairy, please we need your help!
Would you go tell Jackson's dad
That Jackson has a cavity
That's getting really bad."

So the Tooth Fairy then whispered,
"Wake up, I have some news."
But Doodles then surprised her,
And dad continued with his snooze.

The Tooth Fairy returned and said,
"I could not wake his father up.
 I startle rather easily
 And got scared off by his pup."

A few more weeks had passed
And Jackson chewed a sandwich when
Suddenly he said, "Hey mom,
I have a loose front tooth again.

"Maybe I can pull this out
Just like the one before."
"You did what?" asked Jackson's mom.
"Oh yes, I tied it to a door."

"Well Jackson, go try on your clothes,
It is family picture night.
And please don't tie loose teeth to doors,
It gives me quite a fright!"

"I would like to get this loose tooth out,
But mom said no doors and string."
So Jackson asked,
"Hey Doodles, can you think of anything?"

Doodles stood, his rear end wagging,
So Jackson thought and said,
"Great idea, Doodles.
We will use your tail instead."

Jackson grabbed some doggie cookies
And headed for the yard.
"With Doodles' help this tooth will pop.
It shouldn't be that hard."

Jackson said to Doodles,
"I'll throw the cookie and you fetch.
That will give the string tied to your tail
Just the perfect stretch."

"Hold it," said the wiggly tooth,
"We can't let them pull me out.
Jackson needs to see his dentist,
That is without a doubt.

"When his dentist sees a wiggly tooth,
The cavity she'll also spot.
She'll fix the hole in our molar friend.
This is our only shot."

"Go fetch!" shouted Jackson
As the cookie flew away.
But just then with his biggest voice,
The loose tooth shouted, "Stay!"

And wow, would you believe it?
Doodles stopped right there and then.
So Jackson pulled another cookie out
And shouted, "Fetch!" again.

But this time all of Jackson's teeth
Yelled, "Stay!" with all their might.
And Doodles didn't move an inch
Much to their delight.

Jackson said, "I thought that
Cookies were your favourite treat?"
Well, Jackson wasn't one to quit
And just accept defeat.

So he said, "I'll just grab this tooth
And give it one more try."
"Oh well," said the wiggly tooth,
"I guess this means goodbye."

"Wait!" said the Dribble Slobber Glands.
"We're turning on the taps.
Taking out this baby tooth
May not be such a snap."

So saliva flowed like a river
And Jackson couldn't get a grip.
And every time he grabbed the tooth,
All it would do is slip.

He tried to move it back and forth
And turn it all about.
But it became too sore to touch,
So he left it sticking out.

Jackson's mom stopped by his room.
"Do your good clothes fit alright?
Whoa, what happened to your tooth?
It is sure is quite a sight."

"I tried to take it out myself
But the tooth got wet and slippy."
"Well, it looks just awful," his mother said.
"No mom, it's just a little tippy."

"We can't take a family pic tonight
With a baby tooth like that.
Let me take it out for you,
I'll be done in seconds flat."

"No mom, please don't touch it.
I made it really sore."
"Well, then let's call the dentist.
This problem's one we can't ignore."

"Come in, Jackson," said the dentist.
"I am a dental sleuth.
Because I never miss a cavity
Like the one in your back tooth.

"Don't worry we can fill it,
It will be good as new.
And let's take out that wiggly tooth.
It looks quite overdue."

So the dentist did save Jackson's tooth.
The filling looked just fine.
And as for Jackson's wiggly tooth,
The Tooth Fairy returned that night at 9.

So all the teeth in Jackson's mouth
Were happy big and small.
And Jackson's family got their
Picture taken after all.

Dear Reader,

We hope you enjoyed reading this story as much as Catherine Lee and I enjoyed creating it.

Did you know that Saving Jackson's Tooth started out as a non-rhyming story? If you would like to download the free e-book featuring the non-rhyming version of "Saving Jackson's Tooth," please visit my author website DrJeffShnall.com for details.

My author website will let you know when I release new books and will keep young readers updated on what Jackson, Mia, Doodles and, of course, Jackson's teeth are up to.

If you would like to see other works by illustrator Catherine Lee and keep updated about what she is up to, please visit her website walnutandclam.wordpress.com for details.

Jeff Shnall

Acknowledgements

I would like to thank my many enthusiastic patients who read drafts of this book to their children and gave me very useful feedback on areas to improve the story.

A warm thanks as well to Cathie Gillespie, Marie Lardino, Patricia Daigneault and all the other staff at Voice Integrative School (VIS) in Toronto for their support and interest in this book.

I am particularly grateful to VIS English teacher Kristin McCullough and her Grade 7 and 8 students who gave me insightful critiques that resulted in some important additions and deletions to the poem and pictures.

To the amazingly talented Catherine Lee – my immense gratitude for doing such a wonderful job illustrating this book and its cover, for making the characters I envisioned come to life and for making me believe that teeth can actually talk!

To Edee Lemonier and Alison Choi, my appreciation for your vital editorial help.

A big thank you to my dental office staff, who shared in my excitement in producing this book and whose dedication makes me look forward to coming to work each day.

A heartfelt thank you to all of my patients, who are an honour to treat and who make me happy that I chose to become a dentist.

And a final thank you to my partner in life Alison Choi, to my kids Joanna, Laura and Ben and my mom Arlene, who are my biggest supporters. This book is dedicated to you.

Jeff Shnall

Manufactured by Amazon.ca
Bolton, ON

28187467R00026